CAN YOU
IMAGINE?

Being a
BULLFROG

By Jagger
Youssef

Gareth Stevens
Publishing

Please visit our website, www.garethstevens.com. For a free color catalog of all our high-quality books, call toll free 1-800-542-2595 or fax 1-877-542-2596.

Library of Congress Cataloging-in-Publication Data

Youssef, Jagger.
Being a bullfrog / by Jagger Youssef.
 p. cm. — (Can you imagine)
Includes index.
ISBN 978-1-4339-9860-7 (pbk.)
ISBN 978-1-4339-9861-4 (6-pack)
ISBN 978-1-4339-9858-4 (library binding)
1. Bullfrog — Juvenile literature. I. Title.
QL668.E27 Y68 2014
597.892—dc23

First Edition

Published in 2014 by
Gareth Stevens Publishing
111 East 14th Street, Suite 349
New York, NY 10003

Copyright © 2014 Gareth Stevens Publishing

Designer: Katelyn E. Reynolds
Editor: Therese Shea

Photo credits: Cover, p. 1 outdoorsman/Shutterstock.com; cover, pp. 1–32 (background texture) AnnabelleaDesigns/Shutterstock.com; pp. 4, 20 JIANG HONGYAN/Shutterstock.com; p. 5 Ilias Strachinis/Shutterstock.com; p. 7 E. R. Degginger/Photo Researchers/Getty Images; p. 8 Dan Suzio/Photo Researchers/Getty Images; p. 9 Edward Kinsman/Photo Researchers/Getty Images; p. 11 Hemera/Thinkstock.com; pp. 13 (all), 21 iStockphoto/Thinkstock.com; p. 15 Gerald A. DeBoer/Shutterstock.com; p. 17 Thomas Marent/Visuals Unlimited, Inc/Getty Images; pp. 19, 29 Photo Researchers/Getty Images; p. 23 © iStockphoto.com/rmarnold; p. 24 David Kay/Shutterstock.com; p. 25 Kenneth H Thomas/Photo Researchers/Getty Images; p. 27 Jupiterimages/Photos.com/Thinkstock.com.

Printed in the United States of America

CPSIA compliance information: Batch #CW14GS: For further information contact Gareth Stevens, New York, New York at 1-800-542-2595.

CONTENTS

Words in the glossary appear in **bold** type the first time they are used in the text.

JUST IMAGINE

Picture yourself with smooth, damp, green skin. You're only about 8 inches (20 cm) long. You like to live in wet places, and you hop and swim to get around. Your favorite meals are bugs, mice, and just about anything you can fit in your very wide mouth. You just imagined yourself as a bullfrog!

What's this large frog's life like? It's not all fun. Like most animals, bullfrogs are just trying to stay alive. Read on to find out more.

imagine that!

Some American bullfrogs are green, while others have gray-brown skin with spots.

The American bullfrog is the largest frog in the United States.

5

STARTING OUT

If you were a bullfrog, you'd begin your life in a tiny egg. Bullfrog eggs don't have hard shells. They have to stay wet, so they're laid in water. A mother bullfrog may lay as many as 20,000 eggs at a time. She doesn't stay with the eggs to **protect** them, though. Fish and other animals eat some of the eggs.

Bullfrog eggs hatch between 5 and 20 days after they're laid. Polliwogs, also called tadpoles, come out. They don't look like frogs. They have tails and **gills**.

imagine that!

If you were a bullfrog, you could have more than 20,000 brothers and sisters!

A mother bullfrog lays her eggs on the surface of a still body of water, such as a pond.

TADPOLES

If you were a bullfrog tadpole, you'd be a greenish color and have dark spots all over your body. Tadpoles grow to be about 6 inches (15 cm) long over 2 years. They eat plants that grow in water.

Slowly, the tadpoles grow lungs as well as front and back legs. Their tail begins to shorten, and their gills disappear. It can take a few years for a bullfrog tadpole to become a young bullfrog, or froglet.

This bullfrog tadpole's head is starting to look a bit like an adult bullfrog's head. Later, it will look more like the bullfrog tadpole on page 8.

9

ALL GROWN UP

As a froglet, you can now hop around on land and breathe air through your lungs. Froglets are even smaller than tadpoles. They're just about 2 inches (5 cm) long. They still have some growing to do, though. They may still have a small tail, too.

As the largest American frogs, bullfrogs grow to be about 8 inches (20 cm) long. Their back, or hind, legs measure about 10 inches (25 cm). These long legs make them excellent jumpers. They can jump about 15 times their body length!

imagine that!

A bullfrog commonly weighs about 1 pound (454 g).

The Life Cycle of a Bullfrog

1 egg
2 tadpole
3 froglet
4 adult

A bullfrog usually lives 7 to 9 years in the wild.

4

3

2

1

11

AMPHIBIANS

You've just read that bullfrogs spend some of their lives in water and some of it out of water. Frogs are **amphibians**, and all amphibians share this feature.

Not all amphibians spend their lives near water once they become adults. Tree frogs, for example, might only return to water to **mate** and lay eggs. Then, they go back to their lives on land. However, bullfrogs are different. They like to be near or in water most of the time.

imagine that!

Frogs have tiny teeth, while toads don't.

12

red-eyed tree frog

Frogs, toads, and salamanders are all amphibians.

salamander

toad

13

HABITATS

Like other amphibians, bullfrogs are cold-blooded. That means their body temperature changes when the temperature around them changes. So if you were a bullfrog, you'd want to live somewhere warm.

The American bullfrog is native to the East Coast, from Canada to Florida. However, its **habitat** is expanding. Bullfrogs can now be found as far west as California. Also, we're not sure how they got there, but American bullfrogs are found in Europe, South America, and Asia, too.

imagine that!

A bullfrog's skin helps it blend in. Would you want **camouflage** like this?

Bullfrogs live in ponds, lakes, and rivers. They like calm, shallow waters.

15

HIBERNATION

Some of the places bullfrogs live get cold during winter. What do the cold-blooded creatures do? If you were a bullfrog, you'd **hibernate** through winter! Bullfrogs hibernate underwater. Their body processes slow down. They don't need to eat, and they need only a small amount of **oxygen** to stay alive.

Hibernating bullfrogs sit in the mud at the bottom of their watery home and take in the oxygen they need from the water. However, they may swim around sometimes.

imagine that!

A hibernating frog may partially freeze during the winter. Its heart may stop. When it thaws, it "comes back to life"!

16

Bullfrogs don't bury themselves completely in mud when they hibernate. They wouldn't be able to breathe.

17

WAITING FOR A MEAL

When the warm weather arrives, bullfrogs come up and are ready to eat! What's for dinner if you're a bullfrog? Imagine eating snakes, worms, bugs, spiders, snails, fish, salamanders—and even other bullfrogs. Yes, bullfrogs eat each other! Unsurprisingly, bullfrogs like to live alone and don't share territory.

Bullfrogs sit still and wait for prey to pass by. When it does, a bullfrog flicks out its sticky tongue and uses it to pull the animal into its mouth. A bullfrog may jump several feet to catch a meal, too.

imagine that!

Bullfrogs live longer in warmer places.

Bullfrogs even eat birds, feathers and all!

19

CALLING ALL BULLFROGS

Bullfrogs may not like each other, but they do **communicate**. They have a deep, loud call that can be heard from a half mile (0.8 km) away. It sounds a bit like the noise that a bull makes, which is how the bullfrog got its name.

A bullfrog's call usually means either "Stay away! This is my territory!" or "I'm looking for a mate!" Bullfrogs mate once a year, from May to July in the North and February to October in the South.

imagine that!

Bullfrogs have even been known to eat bats!

A bullfrog's throat swells like this when it croaks.

PREDATORS!

Like other amphibians, bullfrogs make a toxin, or poison, in their body. It oozes onto their skin and makes them taste bad to many predators. However, bullfrogs still have enemies. Some of bullfrogs' main predators are turtles, snakes, raccoons, and water birds, such as herons, egrets, and kingfishers.

If you were a bullfrog, you'd have an even larger enemy—people. Some people catch bullfrogs because they like to eat bullfrog legs! Certain times of year are set aside for bullfrog hunting.

imagine that!

People catch bullfrogs for another reason: bullfrog racing!

This heron just found its dinner!

23

BOY OR GIRL BULLFROG?

How can you tell a male bullfrog from a female bullfrog? There is a round circle on each side of the frog's head. These are its outer ears. Male bullfrogs have outer ears much larger than their eyes. On female bullfrogs, these circles may look about as large as or smaller than their eyes.

When bullfrogs are ready to mate, it's easy to tell the difference between males and females. The throat of the male bullfrog is yellow, and the female's throat is white.

male bullfrog

The outer ear of a bullfrog is called a tympanum.

female bullfrog

25

BULLFROGS TAKING OVER

Bullfrogs are spreading successfully because they can stay alive in changing conditions. As water becomes warmer due to pollution and other factors, bullfrogs keep **thriving** while other animals get sick. Bullfrogs can also travel several miles to another body of water if they need to, especially in wet weather.

Bullfrog tadpoles are sometimes transported with fish to other areas by accident. When they grow into adult bullfrogs, they eat the native frogs. Some kinds of frogs are in trouble because of bullfrogs taking over their habitats.

imagine that!

Scientists are now thinking of ways to keep bullfrog populations under control, including introducing fish into their habitats that would eat them.

This male bullfrog is chowing down on a smaller frog.

27

BULLFROGS HELPING OUT

Bullfrogs are very good at one activity—eating. That's helpful for people because bullfrogs like to eat animals that we think are pests. If there weren't any bullfrogs, there might be a lot more **mosquitoes**, bugs, mice, and other kinds of animals that annoy people. Bullfrogs keep these troublesome populations low.

So now that you know more about being a bullfrog, would you want to be one? No matter your answer, it's fun to imagine!

imagine that!

Bullfrogs are now found in every US state, including Hawaii.

This bullfrog makes a snack out of a worm. If you were a bullfrog, you'd think a worm was tasty!

29

GLOSSARY

amphibian: an animal that spends time on land but has babies and grows into an adult in water

camouflage: an animal's colors or shape that allow it to blend in with its surroundings

communicate: to give or receive information through noise, writing, or movement

gill: the body part that water-dwelling animals such as fish use to breathe in water

habitat: the natural place where an animal or plant lives

hibernate: to be in a sleeplike state for an extended period of time, usually during winter

mate: to come together to make babies. Also, one of two animals that come together to make babies.

mosquito: a small fly that feeds on the blood of some animals and can spread illness

oxygen: a colorless, odorless gas that most animals, including people, need to breathe

protect: to guard

thrive: to grow in good health

FOR MORE INFORMATION

Books

Gray, Susan H. *Bullfrog*. Ann Arbor, MI: Cherry Lake Publishing, 2009.

Rustad, Martha E. H. *Bullfrogs*. Minneapolis, MN: Jump!, 2014.

Websites

American Bullfrog
animals.nationalgeographic.com/animals/amphibians/american-bullfrog/
Hear what a bullfrog sounds like.

American Bullfrog
www.arkive.org/american-bullfrog/lithobates-catesbeiana/
See amazing photos of a bullfrog's life.

Bullfrogs Eat Everything
video.nationalgeographic.com/video/animals/amphibians-animals/frogs-and-toads/frog_bull/
Watch this video about a bullfrog's big appetite.

INDEX